For Sebastien and Mae,
who always bring sunshine to my life

Text and illustrations copyright © 2018 by Jami Gigot

First Edition 2018

Library of Congress Control Number 2017942478
ISBN 978-0-9990249-0-4

2 4 6 8 10 9 7 5 3 1
Printed in China

This book was typeset in Kiddish.
The illustrations were rendered in pencil and digital paint.
Book designed by Jami Gigot

Ripple Grove
Press

Portland, Oregon
RippleGrovePress.com

SEB
AND THE
SUN

BY JAMI GIGOT

Ripple Grove
Press

Seb lived in a sleepy coastal town far in the north.
So far north that the sun did not shine in winter
and the days were cold, dreary, and dark as night.

Seb missed the sun.

To pass the time, Seb combed the beach for treasures.
His friend Walrus was an excellent treasure finder, even in the dark.
"It's perfect for my collection!" said Seb.

Seb and Walrus shared a honey sandwich with the crust cut off.

"I wonder where the sun could be," thought Seb.
Walrus only bellowed, wanting another sandwich.

When Seb's toes were too cold to wiggle,
he knew it was time to head home.

On his way, he passed the miners as they clutched their steaming
mugs of coffee and hot soup.
He waved to Mrs. Vandermuss, who knit furiously by a roaring fire.

He nodded to old Bruce Brewster, who put on a second pair of gloves.
He said hello to Mr. and Mrs. Muktuk, who assured him they would
finish the carving by summer.

Seb peered out into the day that was dark as night
and dreamed of warmer, sunnier times.

He wondered if there was a way to bring the sun
back to his sleepy coastal town, even for a moment.

That night Seb made a plan . . .

and the next day he got straight to work.

The first thing he needed was rope—lots and lots of rope.

The miners had plenty of rope to share.

Mrs. Vandermuss had skeins of yarn.

Old Bruce Brewster gave Seb some fishing line from his tackle box.

Mr. and Mrs. Muktuk had no rope, but they gave him a rusty bucket.

Seb piled everything into his wagon and made his way down to the fjord.

Bit by bit, Seb knotted, looped, twisted, and tied the strands together.
"The sun must be out there," he said.

Walrus snorted excitedly,
and together they boarded a small boat . . .

and rowed far out to sea.

Carefully, Seb untangled the jumble of rope
and tied it to the bucket with a neat barrel hitch.

Then he threw the bucket with all his might.

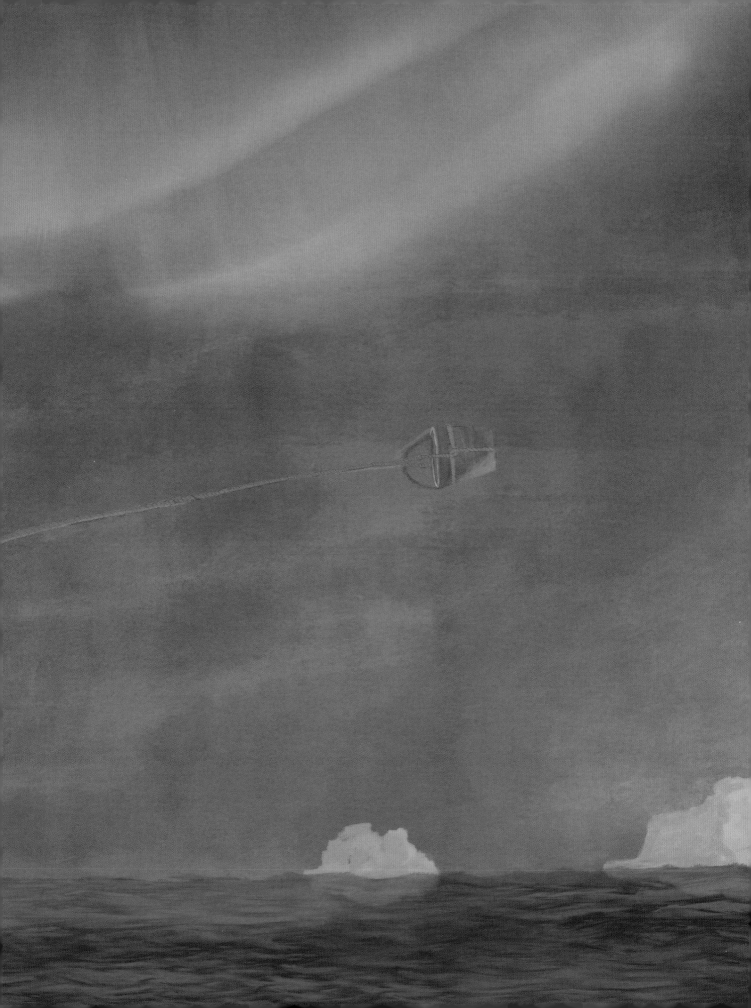

Seb and Walrus waited.

They shared a honey sandwich with the crust cut off

and waited.

Seb's toes were getting too cold to wiggle.
He thought about heading home.

His eyelids grew heavy, and he snuggled close to Walrus.

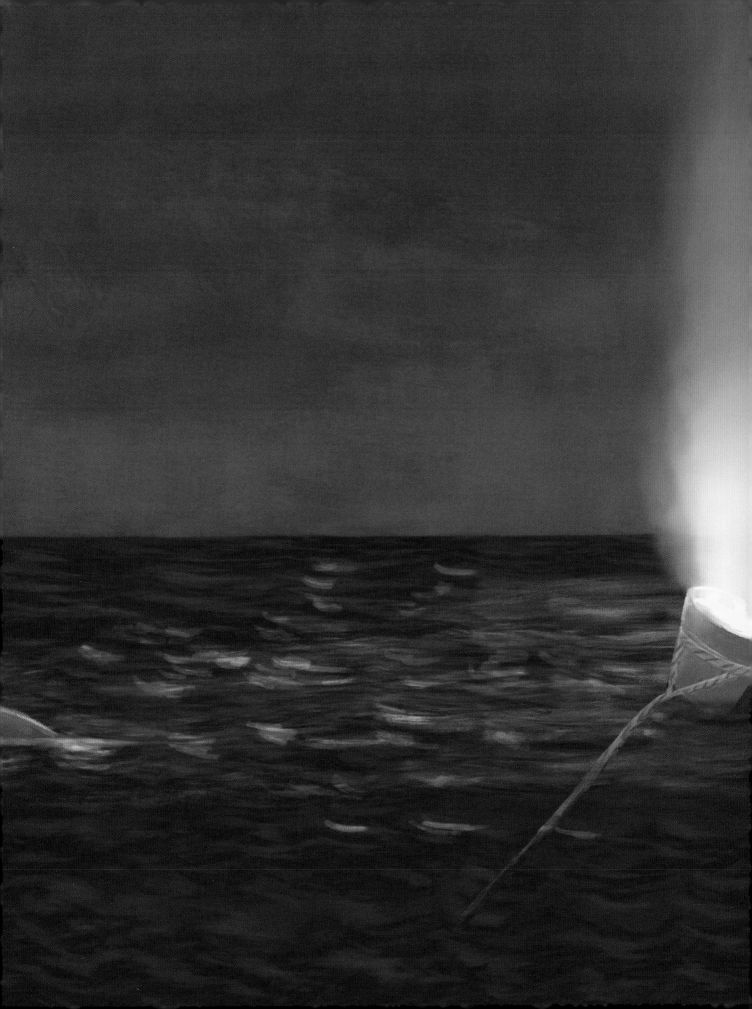

Walrus barked loudly and Seb woke with a start.
"We did it!" shouted Seb.

"Come on, Walrus. I know just what to do."

The townspeople marveled at their warm bottles of sunshine.

Seb's sleepy coastal town was no longer cold, dreary,
and dark as night, but beautifully aglow.

He wiggled his toes.
They were warm.

Walrus only bellowed, wanting another sandwich.